MYSTERY OF
NAVAJO MOON

MYSTERY OF
NAVAJO MOON

Written and Illustrated
By Timothy Green

Northland Publishing

FIRST EDITION
First Softcover Edition, 1993
ISBN 0-87358-523-2 (hardcover)
ISBN 0-87358-577-1 (softcover)
Library of Congress Catalog Card Number 91-52600

Cataloging-in-Publication-Data
Green, Timothy.
    Mystery of Navajo Moon / written and illustrated by Timothy
Green. — 1st ed.
    48p.
    Summary: a young Navajo girl goes on a magical night ride
upon a silvery steed.
    ISBN 0-87358-523-2 (hardcover) : $14.95
    ISBN 0-87358-577-1 (softcover) : $7.95
    [1. Horses—Fiction.   2. Moon—Fiction.   3. Night—Ficton
4. Navajo Indians—Fiction.   5. Indians of North America—Fiction]
1. Title
PZ7.G82636My   1991   91-52600
[E]—dc20   CIP

Manufactured in Hong Kong

For Kristine

ilma Charley
is a Navajo girl. Her home, called
a hogan, is nestled between great
towering mesas, and desert
flowers bloom in bright bouquets
all around it.

One autumn night, the Navajo Moon grew exceptionally large and bright. Wilma awakened to strange sounds outside her window. The wind clattered and howled in a most frightening manner. Dancing junipers rattled in moonlight mischief. Tumbleweeds threw themselves against her window in a terrible fury.

**A**fter awhile,
the wind stopped howling.
Silence hushed the night air.
Wilma crept out of bed and
peered outside her window.
It seemed like the stars twinkled
a little brighter than usual.
Mist blanketed the flowers,
making their petals sparkle.
Softly, drowsiness touched
Wilma's cheek.

ilma awoke
the next morning and wondered
if she had been dreaming. But
she discovered a treasure
glistening outside her window.
The Navajo Moon had
bestowed a gift.
It sparkled in her hand, changing
colors in the morning light.
It felt cold and hard. Wilma had
never in her life seen a
diamond star.

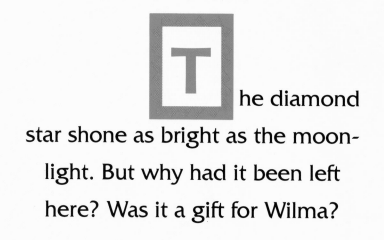

he diamond star shone as bright as the moon-light. But why had it been left here? Was it a gift for Wilma?

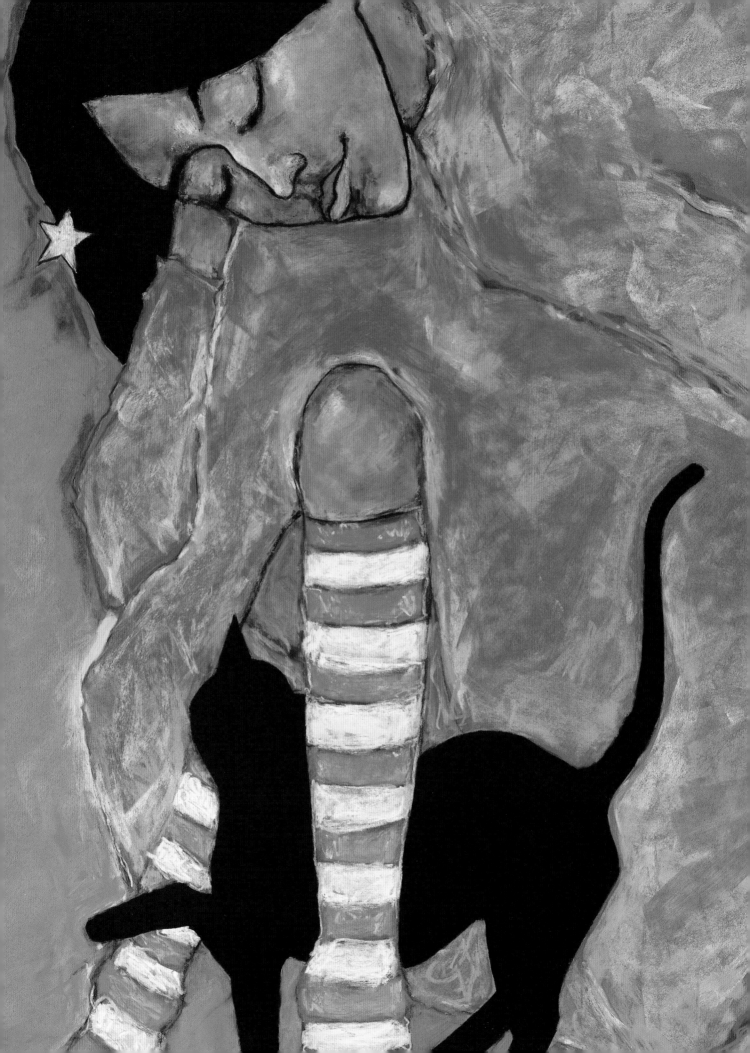

hat night,
she placed the diamond star
beneath her pillow. Dreams soon
filled her eyes. Not a sound could
be heard in the house except for
the gentle breath of slumber.

On the middle of the night, Wilma heard something snap. The wind began to murmur through the trees. An eerie light shone through her window and whispered her name.

"Wilmaaa . . ."

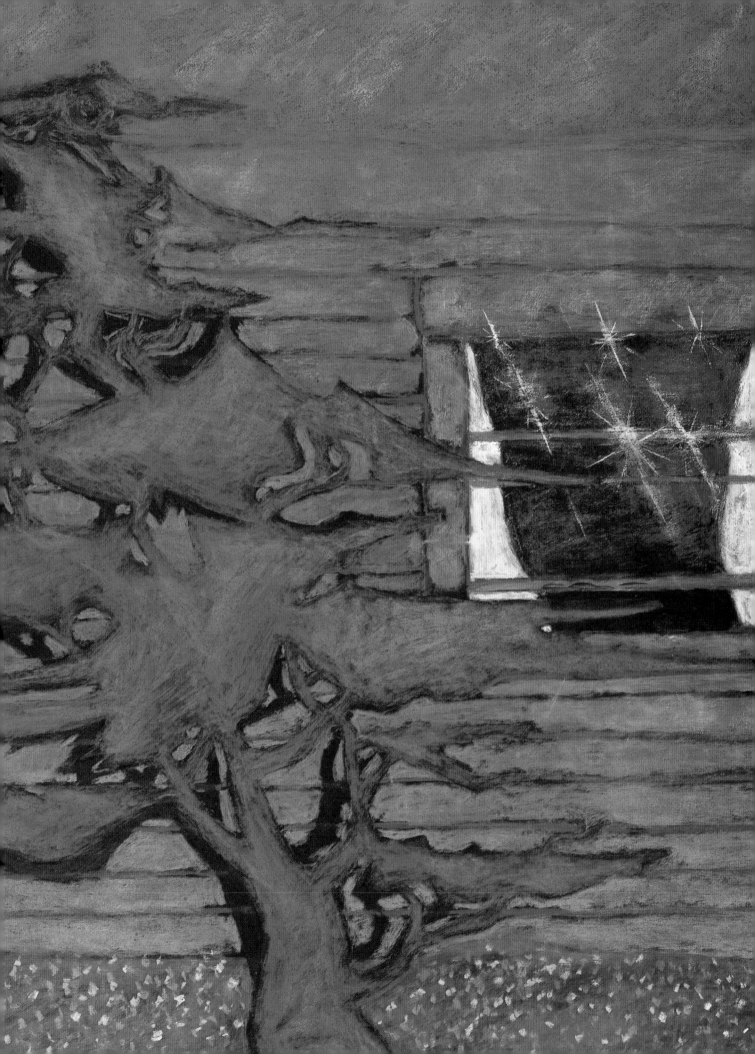

nce again,
Wilma looked out her bedroom
window. The juniper branches
cast strange shadow shapes all
around. Even the ground seemed
to be alive with dancing dark-
ness. Dragonflies twinkled
before her very eyes.
Wilma had to catch her breath at
the beauty before her.

y the light
of a spellbound moon, something
quite marvelous happened!
Outside her window, the most
beautiful pony she had ever seen
appeared before her. The pony
pranced upon the desert flowers.
He was completely white, and
diamond stars sparkled in his
mane. He was a silvery steed of
a thousand dreams.

 ilma could
hardly believe what she saw. She
pinched herself to make sure she
was truly awake!

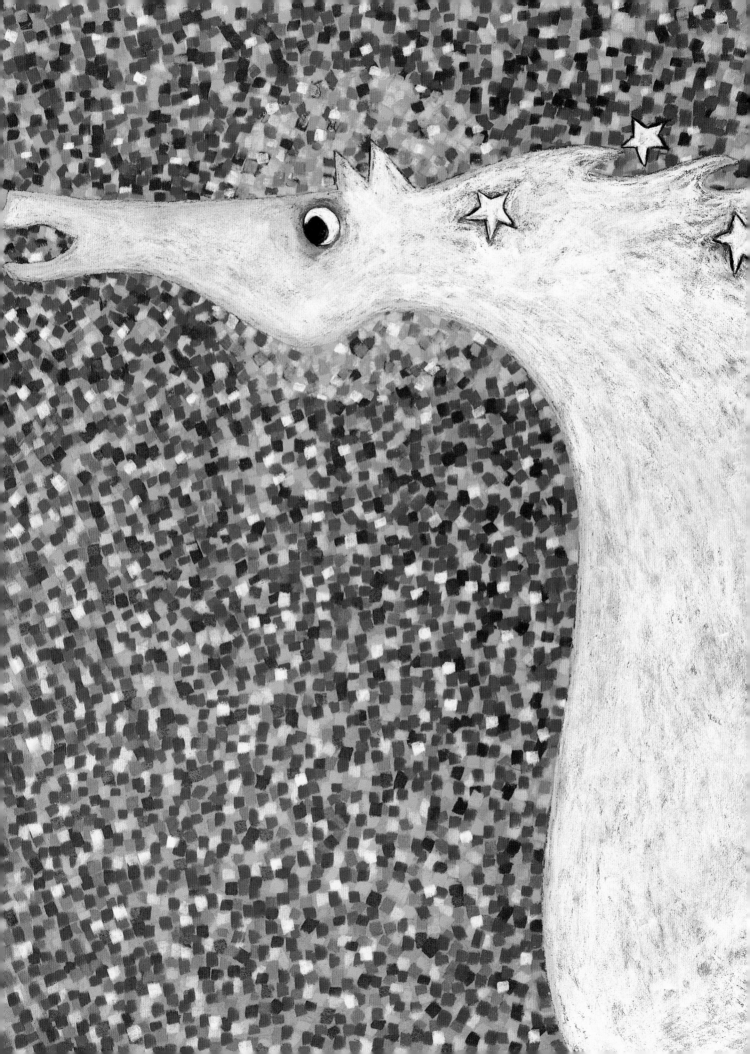

he Navajo Moon beckoned in the night. It whispered to Wilma . . .

fter slipping on her shoes, Wilma climbed out her window—right upon the back of the magnificent pony!

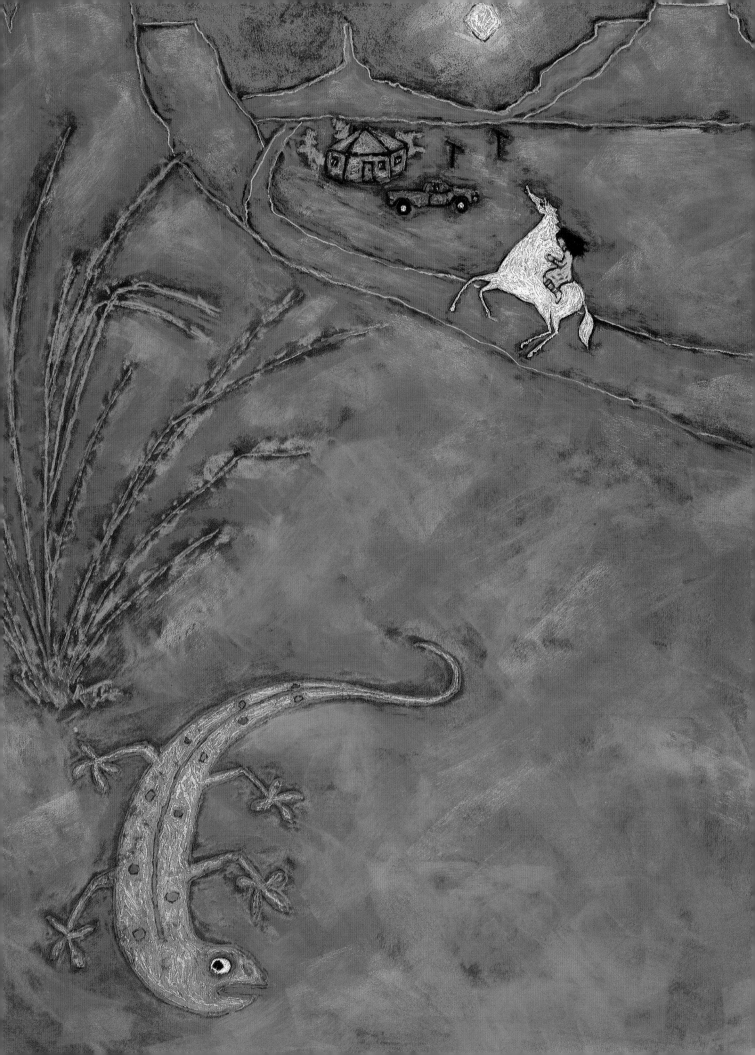

s swift
as lightning, they darted across
the desert. Wilma held on
tightly to the pony's
diamond-starred mane.
Thundering hooves pounded in
her ears. Through wind-blurred
eyes, she could see the ground
rolling away beneath her.
Faster and faster they swept
over sand and sage.

ith a sudden
leap, the pony sprang into the air.
Upward and upward they
bounded toward the stars.

orse and
rider galloped across the sky.
The world below became smaller
and smaller. Soon Wilma was
higher than the hawk-owls
dared to fly.
Wilma and the pony were
silhouetted against the moon.

ith loops
and turns, they circled the earth
below. They raced onward and
forever upward, plunging across
the glittering, vaulted sky.
The heavens were filled with such
splendid things! Candy-colored
moonflakes glimmered like
jewels, swimming amid a sea of
stars. Some looked like
embroidered webs stretched
across the moonlight.

ilma
reached out to grab one . . . .
With a moonflake at her finger-
tips, she suddenly lost her
balance. Before she could utter a
sound, Wilma fell off the pony
and hurtled headlong into the
starlit night.
Falling, falling, falling . . .
Head over heels, she tumbled
downward,
falling,
falling,
falling . . .

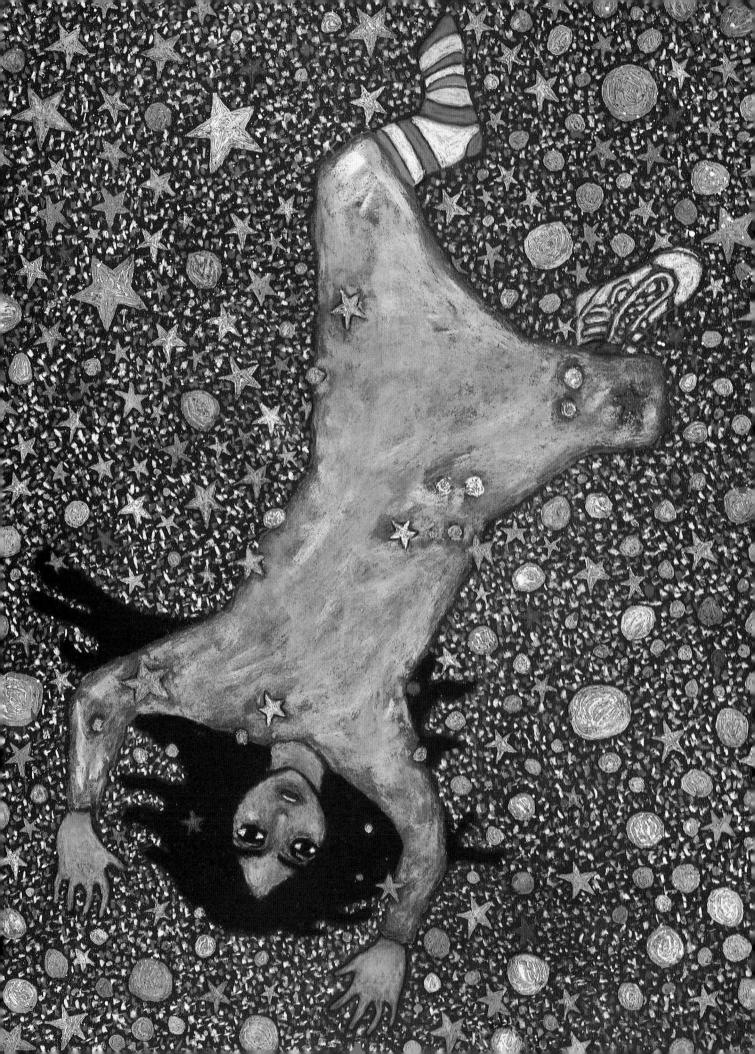

ilma was
awakened in the morning by the
sounds of pots and pans clanging
in the kitchen and the simmering
smells of bacon and frybread.
She was surprised to find herself
back in her warm, cozy bed.
Had she been dreaming?

After
breakfast, Wilma hurried to her
room. The school bus would be
arriving soon and she still
hadn't made her bed.
To her amazement, she found a
new treasure beneath her pillow!
It sparkled like a crystal jewel
embroidered by angels. It was as
delicate as a wisp of dream
breath. It was her very own
moonflake lying beside
her diamond star!

Now, every
night Wilma holds up her
moonflake to the starlight outside
her window. It glows light magic.
She knows that on some en-
chanted night the wonderful pony
will return. Softly, Wilma sings to
the night-mantled heavens . . .
"Oh Navajo Moon,
My secret boon,
Bring to me a gift this night . . .
Bring to me my pony to fly,
And I will hang my moonflake
in the sky."

About the Author

Timothy Green is an artist and educator living on the Navajo Indian Reservation in Arizona with his wife, Kristine; daughter, Dazhoni; two cats; five finches; and numerous stray dogs. He earned his Master of Fine Arts degree in visual art at the University of North Dakota and has exhibited his work extensively. He has taught art at many levels through the North Dakota Artist-in-Residence Program, the Denver School for Gifted Students, and National Endowment for the Arts grants. In addition to *Mystery of Navajo Moon,* he has written a young adult novel, *Mystery of Coyote Canyon* (Ancient City Press).

Designed by Julie Sullivan Scully
Typeset in Friz Quadrata & Lithos